For Joel G. —K.B.
To Liz, my dear friend and fellow logophile —S.S.

Visit us on the Web! rhcbooks.com

Educators and librarians, for a variety of teaching tools, visit us at RHTeachersLibrarians.com

Library of Congress Cataloging-in-Publication Data

Names: Banks, Kate, author. | Shin, Simone, illustrator.

Title: Rumble grumble . . . hush / Kate Banks ; illustrated by Simone Shin.

Description: First edition. | New York : Schwartz & Wade Books, 2017. | Summary: Illustrations and simple, rhyming text follow a little boy

through a day of imaginative play with various toys, followed by a quiet time of books and crayons as bedtime nears.

Identifiers: LCCN 2017007607 (print) | LCCN 2017034114 (ebook) | ISBN 978-1-101-94051-8 (e-book)

ISBN 978-1-101-94049-5 (hardcover) | ISBN 978-1-101-94050-1 (library binding)

Subjects: | CYAC: Stories in rhyme. | Play—Fiction. | Imagination—Fiction. | Toys—Fiction.

Classification: LCC PZ8.3.B2268 (ebook) | LCC PZ8.3.B2268 Rum 2017 (print) | DDC [E]—dc23

The text of this book is set in Belen.

The illustrations were rendered in acrylic paint and digital media.

Book design by Rachael Cole

MANUFACTURED IN CHINA

2 4 6 8 10 9 7 5 3 1

First Edition

RUMBLE GRUMBLE... HUSH

written by Kate Banks • illustrated by Simone Shin

schwartz & wade books • new york

The day starts with a
TICK-TOCK.

A **CLITTER-CLATTER.**

Some **CHITTER-CHATTER.**

A faint MEOW.

A loud

BOW-WOW!

Come on out and play.

A lion gives a mighty roar,
then claps shut an open door
and clips a dragon's wing.

OUCH!

**RAT-A-TAT,
TOOT!
CLING-CLANG!**

A monkey drums and fiddles like a one-man band.

A dump truck empties its load—

RUMBLE

CRUMBLE

BANG!

When suddenly. . .

. . . it's QUIET time.

The quiet drifts in on a current of air

and settles in a tiny chair

and makes itself at home.

Thoughts, they come and go,
words strung in rhythmic rows.
Can a dragon fly with a broken wing?
Can a bear build a house?
Can a monkey sing?

SHUFFLE-SCUFFLE
PITTER-PATTER

HUSH.

SHHH.

The quiet swells and grows.

It creeps around on silent toes.

A little pause.

A quiet hum.

The boy peeks inside

a quiet bag opened wide.

He makes a puzzle

and etches lines

and cuts and
pastes a bright
design.

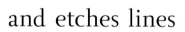

Then he builds a paper house,
the perfect size for a paper mouse.

A book's pages make a breeze,

a quiet shuffle across quiet knees.

Please don't wake the bear.

The boy curls up and takes a nap

with someone cuddled in his lap.

Meanwhile, the cat licks her fur
and dares to utter a gentle PURR
from her cozy perch on the windowsill.

But after the quiet has had its rest,
it leaves the room
like a parting guest.

The quiet bag is put away

in a special place for another day.

Welcome back the sounds, the noise,

rolling balls

and clunky toys.

WHIRRING wheels, a jack-in-the-box,

a **WHISTLING** train,

the **CLIP-CLOP** of blocks.

The **CLINK AND CHINK** of dinner plates
tells the world it's growing late.

Then evening comes with starry eyes.

A bashful moon begins to rise.

But the quiet
that has gone
away

has left a tiny bit to stay.

And when the day is tuckered out,

it lulls the boy to sleep.

Shhh . . . Good night.